✦ ✦ ✦

Adapted by Dandi Daley Mackall

Illustrated by The Krislin Company

Based on the teleplay, *Little Shepherd*, as produced for Lutheran Hour Ministries

✦ ✦ ✦ ✦ ✦ ✦ ✦ ✦

Concordia
Publishing House

Lutheran Hour
Ministries

1   2   3   4   5   6   7   8   9   10   11   10   09   08   07   06   05   04   03   02

Joel chased his little lamb through the hills of Bethlehem. How he longed to be a real shepherd!

"Come on, Bramble!" he called. "Grandfather says you should do as I say, like Father's sheep obey him!"

With a grin and a spin, the little lamb scrambled up the hill.

Meanwhile, Joel's sister, Sarah, listened to stories of wolf sightings. "We'll need every possible shepherd to protect the sheep tonight," her father declared. "Even my Joel."

I should be the shepherd! Sarah thought as she petted a wolf skin in the wagon. *I'd show those wolves a thing or two!*

Then Sarah got an idea ...

Joel stopped chasing his lamb long enough to catch his breath. "Better get back, Bramble. Mother will be worried."

A sound came from the bushes. *Grr-rr-rr!*

"D-did you hear that?" Joel whispered.

The branches shook. Then a furry figure with the head of a wolf jumped out!

Joel tore down the hill and through the marketplace, toppling water jugs, chicken cages, and anybody too slow to get out of the way. "Help! Wolf!" he cried.

Joel raced to his favorite tree and scrambled up, safely out of reach.

Grandfather ambled over. Sarah shed the wolf skin and handed it to the wolf hunter.

She smiled sheepishly as Grandfather said, "Well, *this* wolf looks a lot like my granddaughter!"

Joel scrambled down from the tree. "I can't wait until I'm so big Sarah can't scare me," he complained.

"Being big won't make you fearless, Joel. But God has promised to send the Messiah to be a shepherd to us. Trusting in *His* promise will give you all the courage you need."

Not that old Messiah promise again!" exclaimed Joel's father.
"*Real* shepherd work will make him fearless. And he starts tonight."

"Ben!" Joel's mother objected. "Do you think he's ready?"

"*Harrumph!*" Sarah exclaimed. Joel knew she'd have given anything
to trade places with him. And as he thought of the night ahead,
he would have given anything to trade places with *her*.

Joel was busy imagining hungry wolves stalking the hills for him when Grandfather walked up.

"This was mine when I was your age," Grandfather said, giving Joel a beautiful, carved shepherd's staff. "And I'd like to give you God's promise too."

Joel listened as Grandfather recited the shepherd psalm he had learned when he was young.

The LORD is my shepherd; I have everything I need ...

Oh how Joel wanted to believe the words and the promise!

"Grandfather? Joel?" called Joel's father. "Time to go!"

Joel did his best to keep up with the others, but his legs grew wobbly, and his lamb lagged far behind.

"Bramble!" Joel scolded. "Don't make me use my shepherd's st—!" Joel looked around. "Oh, no! I forgot Grandfather's staff!" he cried. He *had* to get Bramble moving somehow.

So Joel broke into a favorite, off-key, silly song that made Bramble's ears perk up. Sheep scurried out of their way as Joel caught up with his father.

"Stop that noise!" Father scolded. "You're scaring the sheep." He turned to his flock. "Move out!" And the sheep obeyed.

Joel knew he'd never be as good a shepherd as his father. Frustrated, he wheeled on Bramble. "Move it!" he shouted in his father's voice. "You heard me!"

Bramble hung his head and walked away.

Joel felt like crying. No doubt about it. He *was* the worst shepherd in the world.

Joel ran after Bramble, catching up to him up by a bush.
"I'm sorry, Bram—!"

A bone-chilling howl came from the bush. The branches shook.
Joel couldn't move. He opened his mouth, but nothing came out.
Then out of the bushes jumped ... Sarah.

Grandfather came running. "Sarah, wolves are serious business!
And *you* have no business out here!"

"Well, Joel forgot this!" Sarah said as she pulled out a shepherd's staff.

Grandfather didn't look convinced. "Well, it's too late to send you home nov

"Oh, okay," Sarah said, a gleam in her eye. Joel knew Sarah had gotten
exactly what she wanted.

Night fell, and the shepherds settled in to guard their flocks. Suddenly a bright light shone around them. The heavens opened, and an angel appeared, announcing:

To you is born this day in the city of Bethlehem a Savior, your Messiah, who is Christ the Lord. This will be a sign for you. You will find a baby wrapped in cloth and lying in a manger.

Joel turned to Grandfather. "What does it mean?"

"The Messiah has come, just as God promised!" Grandfather exclaimed. "We must all go to Bethlehem!"

The shepherds agreed—all except Joel's father.

"Don't be afraid to believe, Benjamin," Grandfather said.

Benjamin scoffed. "I'm not afraid of anything! I'll come with you just to prove you wrong."

We'll leave the sheep in their pens at home," Benjamin said, "then make our way to Bethlehem."

"Mother can come with us!" Sarah suggested.

"She'll like that," Grandfather agreed. He glanced back at Joel, who was tugging on Bramble. "Hurry, Joel! You don't want to fall behind!"

Joel hurried to catch up, but when he turned, Bramble wasn't there.
"B-a-a! B-a-a!"

Joel followed the sound until he spotted the lamb, tangled in dead branches and stumbling backward toward the edge of the cliff.

"I'm here!" Joel shouted. Then he reached out his staff and pulled Bramble to safety.

Exhausted, Joel flopped down in the soft grass. "Do you think the manger will be golden, Bramble?" He yawned as he snuggled against a rock.

Joel drifted to sleep, dreaming of the Messiah, the stable, and the manger...

Joel woke with a jolt as the wind howled through the hills. How could he have fallen asleep? And where was Bramble?

I'm the worst shepherd ever! Joel thought as he searched in every bush.

Behind him he heard growls. Joel ran to find Bramble surrounded by a pack of snarling wolves.

Joel had to do something. Grandfather's words came to him: *God promises to send us the Messiah to shepherd us. Trusting in His promise will give you courage.* And now the promised Messiah had really come. "I know You are with me," Joel whispered. He stood tall, and in his loudest, off-key voice, started singing.

The wolves turned on Joel. He scrambled over rocks, leading the wolves away from Bramble. Near the cliff's edge, he darted through a hollow log. The wolves snapped at his heels.

Joel leapt to a branch. The wolves lunged after him, diving over the cliff, falling to the valley below. Joel heard them run off yelping.

We did it!" Joel cried as he hugged Bramble.

"Now follow me to Bethlehem."

Joel found his family. Sarah ran up and threw her arms around him.

"I'm sorry for everything, Joel! You have to see Him! He's wonderful!"

"I was so wrong, Joel," said his father.

Grandfather smiled through his tears. "What are you waiting for, Joel?"

Joel and Bramble tiptoed to the manger and peered in at
the amazing baby, wrapped in swaddling clothes. The baby smiled
right at Joel, reached out, and took hold of his finger.

"I wasn't afraid tonight," Joel whispered, feeling the grip of the
tiny fingers, "because I knew You were with me."

His name is Jesus," said Mary, the baby's mother.
She and her husband smiled down at Joel.

Joel saw his father's shawl wrapped around baby Jesus.
More than anything, Joel wished he had a gift for the baby.

Joel stroked Bramble's curly wool. "The only gift I have to give is my lamb."

Bramble stared at his little shepherd, then at baby Jesus, and seemed to understand.

"Bramble's pretty frisky," Joel explained. "But he's a good lamb. Baby Jesus will love him ... like I do."

Joel hurried out of the stable into the arms of his family.

"Where's Bramble?" Sarah asked.

Joel glanced back at the stable. "I gave him to baby Jesus."

His father ruffled his hair. "I'm very proud of you, Son."

Grandfather swiped his eyes with the back of his wrinkled hand. "Let's all go home."

Wait!" The baby's mother walked out to them. "Joel, will you watch over this lamb for Jesus?"

Bramble trotted out from behind her. Mary laughed as she handed Joel the shepherd's staff. "Baby Jesus needs a good shepherd to watch over Bramble."

"I'll be the best shepherd you ever saw!" he cried. "I promise!"

As the sun rose on the hills outside Bethlehem, Joel and his father watched over their flocks.

"Will we see the Messiah again?" Joel asked.

"He will always be with us," Father answered.

Joel knew it. Jesus was the shepherd who would love them so much He would even lay down His own life. He was everybody's shepherd.

As they gazed at the sun, Joel smiled and listened to his father echo his grandfather's words:

The LORD is my shepherd; I have everything I need. He lets me lie down in green meadows.

He leads me beside peaceful streams... He renews my strength...